ZONDERKIDZ

Goodnight, Ark
Copyright © 2014 by Laura Sassi
Illustrations © 2014 by Jane Chapman

This title is also available as a Zondervan ebook.
Visit www. Zondervan.com/ebooks

Requests for information should be addressed to:

Zonderkidz, 3900 *Sparks Dr. SE, Grand Rapids, Michigan* 49546

Library of Congress Cataloging-in-Publication Data

Sassi, Laura, 1969
    Goodnight, Ark / by Laura Sassi.
        pages cm
    Summary: When frightened animals squeeze intoNoah's bed
during a storm, causing the Ark to tip, Noah soothes the beasts
with a lullaby.
    ISBN 978-0-310-73784-1 (hardcover)
    1. Noah's ark—Juvenile fiction. [1. Stories in rhyme. 2. Noah's
ark—Fiction. 3. Bedtime—Fiction. 4. Animals—Fiction.] I. Title.
PZ8.3.S237Go 2014
[E]—dc23   2013033152

Editor: Barbara Herndon
Art direction and design: Cindy Davis

Printed in China

14 15 16 /DSC/ 10 9 8 7 6 5 4 3 2 1

For my two little monkeys
—L. S.

Dedicated to Joshua, Miriam, Stephen, Jacob,
Daniel, Luke, and Ariella
—J. C.

Goodnight, Ark

written by **Laura Sassi**

illustrated by **Jane Chapman**

ZONDER**kidz**

Beds are ready.
Food is stored.
Noah hollers,

"All aboard!"

Guests rush forward.
Furry, scaled,
woolly, feathered,
swishy-tailed.

"Time for bed.
It's getting dark.
Find your buddy
on the ark."

Two by two
to bed they creep.
Noah yawns.
"It's time to sleep."

Then ...

Pitter-pat!
It rains. It pours.
Noah sleeps,

but not ...

THE BOARS!

Grunting, groaning.
Bam! Wham! Scram!
Into Noah's
bed they cram.

Pop! Pop! Ping! Ping!
Pelting hail
pounds the rooftop.

Wakes ...

THE QUAIL!

Flapping, flying,
up they zoom.
Squee! Squee! Squawk!
To Noah's room.

Zip! Zing! Lightning
spooks the sheep.
Baah! They run and
join the heap.

Crash! Boom! Rumble!
Thunder quakes.

Wakes the ...

ELEPHANTS

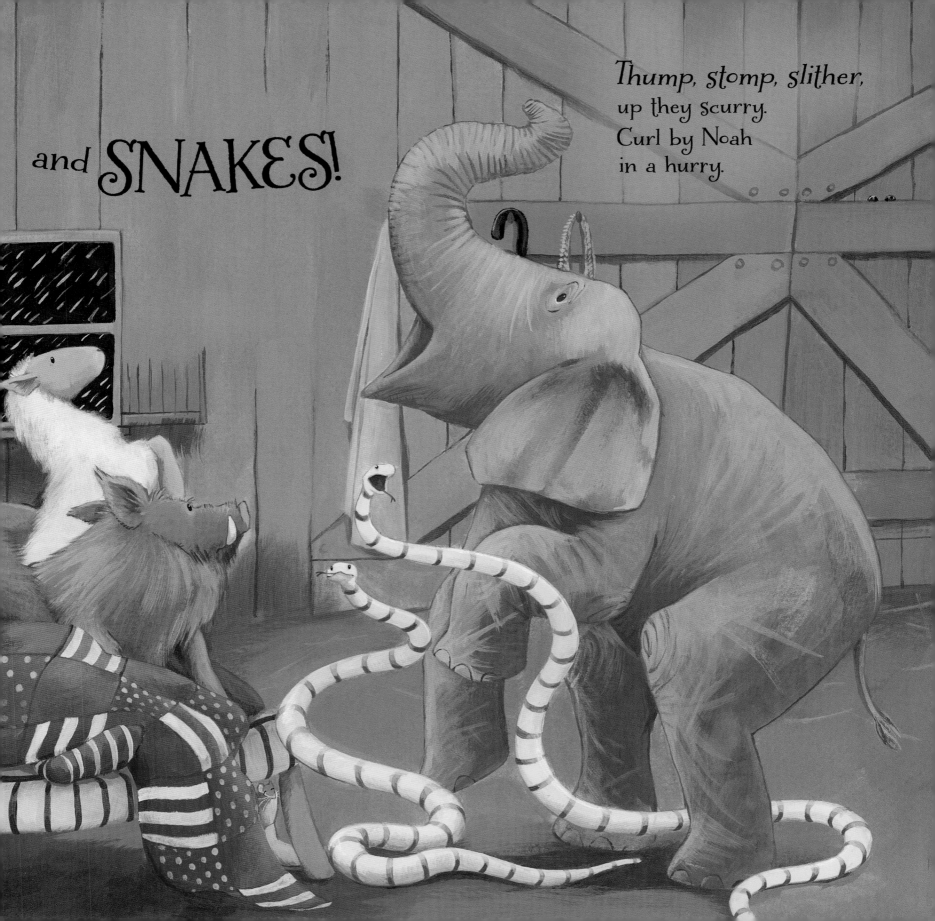

and SNAKES!

Thump, stomp, slither,
up they scurry.
Curl by Noah
in a hurry.

Rain, rain, more rain—
Ark's afloat!
Nervous tigers
rock the boat.

Pouncing, pawing,
up they dash.
Into Noah's
bed they crash.

Now ...

Ark is tipping!
Tip, slip, slide!
Noah wakes up
as they glide.

Faster! Faster!
Rumble! Shake!
"Watch out or

this bed will ...

Snorting nostrils,
blaring trunks,
tumbling riders

startle ...

Pee-ew! Stinky!
Fumes are thick!
Back to bunks now

double-quick!

Softly, Noah
starts to croon
a soothing, sleepy
nighttime tune.

Whoosh! The wind
begins to howl.
This time not one
beast or fowl ...

makes a single
squeak or peep,
for all are snuggly—
fast asleep.

Noah smiles
in the dark.

"Goodnight, friends."
"Goodnight, Ark."